Also by Jane Schoenberg

The One and Only
Stuey Lewis

STUEY LEWIS AGAINST all ODDS

JANE SCHOENBERG

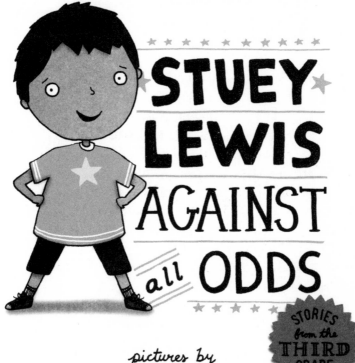

STUEY
LEWIS
AGAINST
all ODDS

STORIES from the THIRD GRADE

pictures by
CAMBRIA EVANS

Margaret Ferguson Books
Farrar Straus Giroux
New York

"The Man on the Moon" song lyrics on page 28
written by Jane Schoenberg

Farrar Straus Giroux Books for Young Readers
175 Fifth Avenue, New York 10010

Distributed in Canada by D&M Publishers, Inc.
Printed in the United States of America by
RR Donnelley & Sons Company, Harrisonburg, Virginia
1   3   5   7   9   10   8   6   4   2

mackids.com

Library of Congress Cataloging-in-Publication Data
Schoenberg, Jane, 1952–
    Stuey Lewis against all odds : stories from the third grade /
Jane Schoenberg ; pictures by Cambria Evans.
        p.   cm.
    Summary: Third-grader Stuey Lewis navigates the ups and
downs of school and family life.
    ISBN 978-0-374-39901-6
    [1. Schools—Fiction.   2. Family life—Fiction.]   I. Evans,
Cambria, ill.   II. Title.   III. Title: Against all odds.

PZ7.S3652St 2012
[Fic]—dc22
                                                      2011008224

For Sarah and Adam, with all my love —J.S.

For Lola and Silas —C.E.

Contents

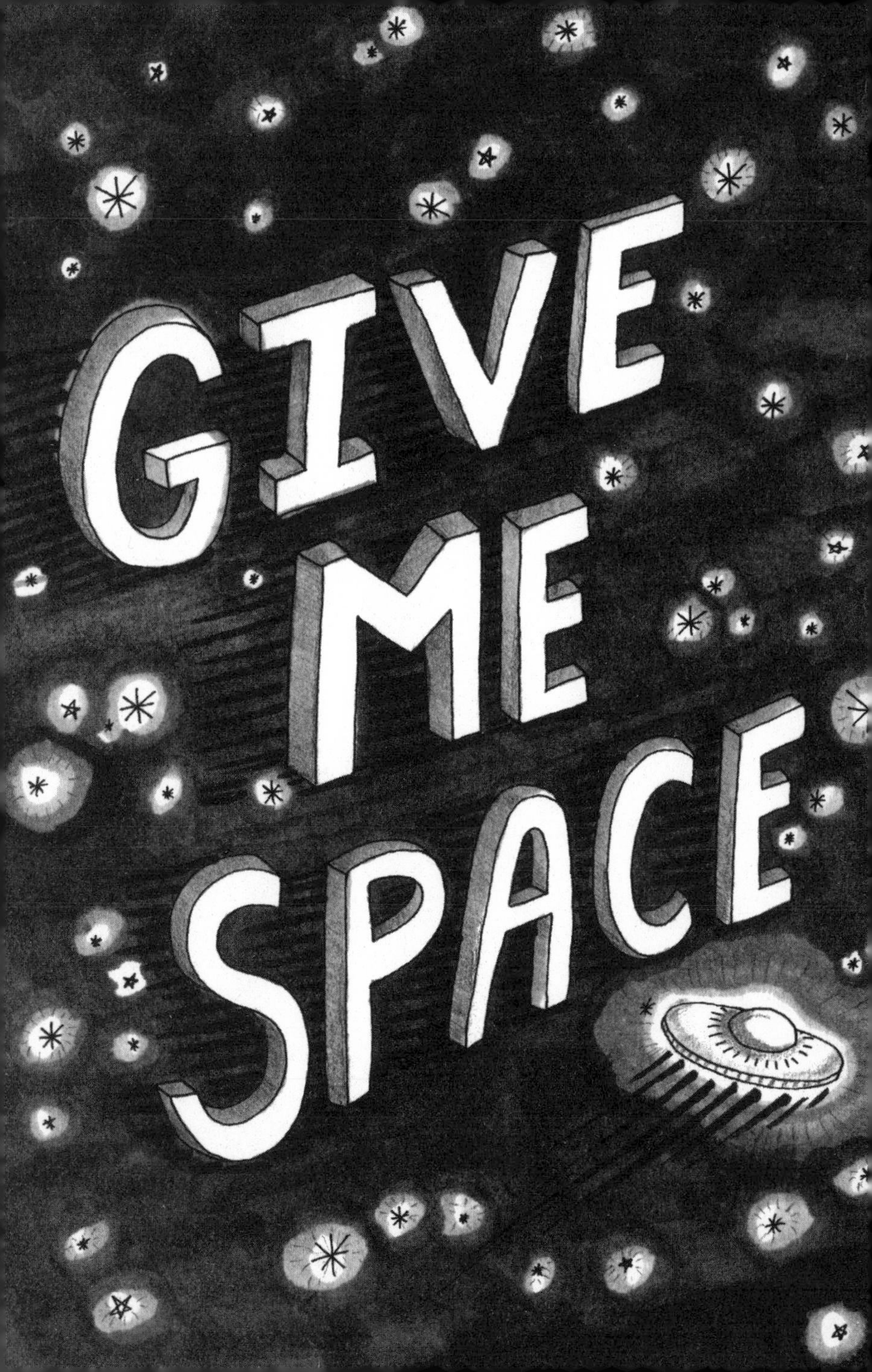
GIVE ME SPACE

Fuel tanks full . . . Booster rockets set . . . Crew standing by . . . Systems are all cleared and ready to go. Prepare to launch," I tell Will Fishman, my best friend and first mate.

One of the coolest things about third grade, besides having Ginger Curtis as our teacher for the second year in a row, and studying space, is having a humongous table full of Legos in our classroom.

"Five, four, three, two, one, zero . . . *Lift off!*" me and Will shout together as our spacecraft leaves the launchpad and quickly soars upward.

Our mission:

* ★ To explore the mysteries of the cosmos.
* ★ To discover new life-forms on other planets.
* ★ To dare to go where no one's ever gone before.

"Ginger! Stuey and Will have been at the Lego table for eighteen and a half minutes now, and there are only ninety seconds of morning recess left. Plus, they've used up all the rocket pieces from the new Lego set, so no one else can make a spaceship."

And one of the worst things about third grade, besides tons of homework and having to learn cursive, which I stink at, is that I *still* have to put up with having the Queen of Obnoxious in my class. I cross my eyes and look at Lilly Stanley. She has two heads and four eyes. Blab-blab-blabs are coming out of her two mouths, and she has morphed into the most annoying alien ever known to humankind in *any* galaxy.

I pick up my Lego laser and wave it at her.

"You know you're not allowed to make guns at school, Stuey Lewis," she blabs on.

"It's not a gun," Will explains. "It's a frezlien, a highly specialized tool designed to freeze aliens for five minutes, without causing bodily harm, while we collect scientific data from them."

"I guess you and I are safe then, Lilly," says Ms. Curtis, chuckling. "Nice-looking rocket, guys. I'm glad you're psyched about our space unit. We'll talk more

about what we'll be studying later, dur-
ing science. Lilly, I bet if it's still raining,
the boys will be happy to have you join
them at the Lego table after lunch. Isn't
that right, Stuey?" she asks me.

"The forecast said there's a seventy
percent chance of the rain ending before

appears. "How about a game of Martian freeze tag?" I call, heading outside to the playground.

"You're IT!" Omar yells to me over his shoulder. I take off across the playing field after him. Before long our entire class is either frozen stiff or racing around. Then Lilly's IT.

"I wish I had your frezlien, Stuey!" she yells, just missing me.

"Lucky for me, you don't," I holler back.

After recess, Ms. Curtis meets us at the classroom door.

"Welcome to Lunar Station, space explorers. Please join me in the control room."

Whoa . . . While we were outside, Ms. Curtis transformed the entire meeting area into a scene from *Star Trek*. All the shelves are filled with space books, and

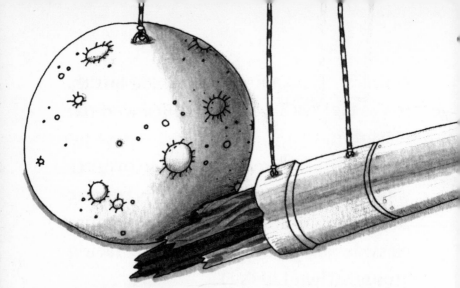

a ginormous rocket and moon are hanging from the ceiling.

"Awesome!" says Sashi, scoping out the rocket. "I've always wanted to go to the moon."

"Who can tell me the name of the first American woman astronaut who traveled in space?" Ms. Curtis asks.

"I know! I know!" Lilly's hand shoots up faster than the speed of light. "Sally Ride," she shouts out. "I know all about her, she was on the space shuttle *Apollo*."

"Sally Ride *was* the first American woman in space, but she flew her two missions on the space shuttle *Challenger*, not *Apollo*," I say. "On the second mission, Kathryn Sullivan was part of her crew, and *she* was the first American woman to ever walk in space."

"I didn't know that about Kathryn Sullivan," says Ms. Curtis. "I love it when I learn things from you guys. What else can someone tell me about space?"

"It has moons and gazillions of stars," says Nathan.

"And planets, too," says Omar.

"There are eight planets in our solar system," Will adds.

"There used to be nine," I say. "But the IAU officially downgraded Pluto to a dwarf planet, so now there's just Mercury, Venus, Earth, Mars, Jupiter, Saturn, Uranus, and Neptune."

"The IA who?" Will asks.

"I-A-*U* . . . as in International Astronomical Union," I tell him.

Everyone stares at me like I'm Bill Nye the Science Guy, from TV.

"How come you know so much about space, Stuey?" Rosa asks.

"His dad runs a space-science center," Will says without thinking.

"Cool! Can we go there on a field trip and have him show us stuff?" Sashi asks me.

I check out Will's face, which is now

the same color as Jupiter's great red spot.

"Sam, we haven't heard from you," Ms. Curtis says, saving me from having to answer Sashi. "What can you tell us about space?"

"Well, there're definitely UFOs flying around up there."

"You've been watching way too much sci-fi, Sam Baker, because UFOs just don't exist," Lilly says.

"Try telling that to my grandpa. He saw one a long time ago."

"No way. Honest, Sam?" Nathan asks. "What did it look like?"

Suddenly, UFO stories start whizzing around the classroom. It gets so noisy no one notices that the "space expert's" mouth is muzzled. Except for Will, who gives me a look that says, Sorry I blew it.

Okay, so lots of kids have parents who are divorced. No biggie if they live close by, but when they don't, it can be a major drag. Dad knows tons about space. It would be wicked cool for him to talk to my class, like Omar's dad did when it was fire-prevention week and we visited his fire station. Or like Sashi's grandpa, who cooked treats with us at his restaurant on Chinese New Year's last year. Problem is, Dad's space center is 1,000 miles away in Georgia.

But hey, if they can figure out a way to get people 238,855 miles to the moon, I should be able to figure something out, right? 'Cause who else happens to be the number-one problem solver on the planet?

When I get home, my big brother, Anthony, is in the kitchen.

"We're studying space," I tell him. "I wish Dad could speak to the class."

"Wish for something else, Stu. Dad already visited this summer."

"Duh, I know he can't come here, but I think I've hatched a plan that will get us all there."

"You've got to be kidding. Take a field trip to Georgia? Earth to Stuart Lewis, come in Stu-pid . . . No one, not even *you* can pull that off. So do yourself a favor, don't mention it to anyone else, 'cause they'll think you're even more of a space cadet than you are."

And just because he calls me stupid, I let him believe I am . . . At least for the moment, anyway. And then I decide to run my plan by Ms. Curtis. She lives around the block from us, so I walk over to her house, where she's outside raking leaves. I fill her in on my scheme, and do you know what? She doesn't think I'm stupid at all.

"Anthony says I'm nuts to believe we could pull off a class trip to Georgia," I tell Will on the phone after dinner. "Do you?"

"Sam's grandpa thinks he saw a UFO. Is he nuts?"

"Lilly thinks so," I answer.

"I rest my case," Will says.

And that's why I immediately swear him to secrecy and share my Teleporta Plan . . . the plan that will transport me and him and Ms. Curtis and our entire third-grade class to Georgia, a thousand miles away. In the blink of an eye . . . No lie.

"Wow, that's incredible," Will says. "I'm in."

Then I tell Mom and call Dad, and swear them to secrecy, too.

"Dad, Ms. Curtis needs to ask Ms. Katz, our principal, if Friday night is okay. She's just waiting to get the go-ahead from you. Can you give her a call now?"

"Will do. I'll go over everything with her so she can get set up on your end," Dad says. "We'll synchronize the rendezvous for eight thirty sharp on Friday night, after everyone clears out of the center, okay, captain?"

"Over and out," I answer.

The next morning, Ms. Curtis has us gather in the meeting area.

"Friends, I have a big surprise. This Friday night, we're all going to have an adventure together that's—"

"You said Friday *night* when you

meant to say Friday *morning*, Ginger," Lilly interrupts. "But don't worry, I get confused sometimes when I'm excited, too."

Ms. Curtis's cheeks turn as red as planet Mars. "Thank you, Lilly, but Friday *night* is exactly what I meant," she says in her most patient voice.

"Ooh," Lilly says, "a *nighttime* adventure. That sounds fascinating. Hurry up and tell us the details."

I give Ms. Curtis a look that says, I know *exactly* how you're feeling.

"Well, I can only talk about the first part of the surprise," she continues, "because that's almost all I know. The details will be revealed that night."

"What *can* you tell us?" Rosa asks.

"That I called Ms. Katz and each of your parents last night and got permission for everybody to stay here at school for a campout."

"How come my mom didn't tell me you called?" Lilly asks.

Before I can stop myself, I hear my not-so-patient voice say, "Because Ginger asked her not to."

"How do *you* know, Stuey Lewis?" Lilly asks.

"He just guessed," says Will.

"And he guessed right," Ms. Curtis says quickly. "I wanted to tell you all about it myself. We'll have dinner together, sleep outside, and something special will happen that has to do with space."

"I hope we get to see a UFO," says Sam.

"Or extraterrestrials," Omar adds.

Lilly rolls her eyes at them. "Yeah, or maybe we'll all take a midnight rocket ride and eat green cheese with the man in the moon."

"Well, it's a safe bet we won't be eating any green cheese, but for sure somebody will probably cut the cheese," I say.

Everyone laughs and Omar and Sam give me the thumbs-up.

"Stranger things *have* been known to happen on campouts, Lilly," I add. "Especially when there's a new moon, so be prepared for *anything*."

"What's a new moon?" Lilly asks.

"When the moon lines up directly in front of the sun, so it looks like there's hardly any moon at all, and the night sky is real dark. That's when you better have a flashlight to light your way back inside, if you wanna make it to the bathroom in time," I answer.

Everyone cracks up again, except for you-know-who.

"You're gross, Stuey Lewis," she says.

"But he's right, it will be a dark night on Friday," says Ms. Curtis, "so we'll all need to bring flashlights. Let's make a list of other things we'll need."

But if my Teleporta Plan is gonna go smoothly, I've got my own list of things to organize, with way more important stuff to think about than sleeping bags, hot dogs, or Lilly Stanley. And I also have to get Anthony psyched up and on board, because Will and me will definitely need his help to pull this off.

"Well, Stu, you're still the man," Anthony says when I tell him about the plan after we get home from school. "Sorry I doubted you. Pretty impressive scheme. Do you think I can come along for the ride?"

"I was hoping you would," I say.

He grins at me. "It's going to be a blast."

Friday morning I wake up raring to go. Mom's already made muffins for tomorrow's breakfast. She hands me a warm one before pushing me out the door.

"This is it, Stu. Now, don't worry, we're all set to play our parts. I'll be there before dinner with your stuff. I'm so excited to be spending the whole night with you and your class. Better get a move on or you'll miss the bus."

Will meets me at the classroom door. "The final countdown to Teleporta is officially on," he whispers. "Let's synchronize our watches. Everything set for 2030 hours?"

"Yeah, Mom's sneaking Anthony and the tech gear into the library at 1730 hours, then she'll show up outside to help with the cookout. She'll be the gofer between us and Anthony, just like we planned," I whisper back.

"Ginger! Guess what?" we hear Lilly screech from inside the classroom. "You're not the only one with a secret. When my mom comes to help watch us after school, she's bringing something for tonight that everyone's definitely going to love." Then she eyes me. "Just you wait, Stuey, it's the best surprise *ever.*"

I open up my mouth and almost put my foot in it, but Will steps on my toe first. "Keep a lid on it, Stu," he whispers. "We've only got a few hours left."

The day goes by at warp speed. The three o'clock bell rings and everyone's buzzing about tonight. A couple of parents show up and take us outside, where we play space games and asteroid dodgeball. Soon parents start arriving with camping stuff and food that they load on the picnic table. Lilly's mom arrives with a tray piled high with moon pies.

"Moon pies. Get it, Ginger? We used Martha Stewart's recipe but stuffed them with twice as much marshmallow fluff *and* we double-dipped them in chocolate. *And* we made two for each person in the class because they're super yummy and *one* just wouldn't be enough," she blabs on. "And there are extra ones for our parent-helpers, too, so they won't feel left out, because you're never too old to enjoy a good moon pie. So, as you can see, now there are *two* special things about space scheduled for tonight, Ginger . . . your surprise and *my* moon pies."

If moon pies weren't way up there on my dessert list, I'd be throwing up right about now.

"Wow," says Rosa, "those look amazing."

"Bet they taste amazing, too," Nathan adds.

"I'd be happy to pass them out for an after-school snack," Lilly offers.

"I think that's a

great idea." Ms. Curtis smiles. "Why don't you start with Stuey."

"Psst!" Mom signals us over to the place where she's setting up the grill for our hot dogs. She points. "Anthony's just inside that door. He wants to speak to you."

Me and Will rap on the door when no one's looking.

Anthony opens it a crack. "Phase One and Two of the plan are complete," he reports. "Mom put the seats the way you wanted, and I've got us all hooked up. You just have to keep the kids away from the library until takeoff."

"Done," Will says. "My dad's organizing our campsite on the field closest to the school. He was an Eagle Scout. Trust me, having people inside is not on his agenda. Right now he's got everyone setting out their sleeping bags. Then he's taking the kids for a walk on the nature path in the woods before we eat."

"Speaking of dinner, you must be starving," I say to Anthony. "I'll have Mom slip out and bring you a dog as soon as they're ready."

"I'm cool," he says, "but maybe you can score another one of those moon pies for me. Ms. Curtis brought me one earlier and . . ."

"One just wasn't enough?" I guess.

"Oh, you've tried them . . . Pretty awesome, huh?"

"Yeah." I roll my eyes at Will. "Pretty awesome."

When we're all done eating, we sit in a circle on the grass. Ms. Curtis gets her guitar out and launches into *"It was a one-eyed, one-horned, flyin' purple people eater."* I give her a big grin. Just think, I could have ended up with a third-grade teacher who sings "Twinkle, Twinkle."

"It's getting pretty dark out," Omar says, looking up at the sky.

"When is the space surprise happening, Ginger?" Sashi asks.

"Soon," Ms. Curtis says, checking her watch. And then I hear our cue. "We'll have just enough time to read another chapter of *Lost in Space*. Stuey, would you and Will mind getting it for me? It's on my desk."

"I'll get it, Ginger," Lilly says.

"I was hoping you would help me sing. *"Hip-hopping it out to a rocking tune,"* Ms. Curtis sings, strumming. Lilly's voice joins in, *"Is that crazy old, crazy old man on the moon . . ."*

And we're off, making our getaway into school, up the hallway to the library. Mom passes us in the opposite direction, heading outside with an armload of blindfolds.

"Phase Three in progress," she reports. "I'll see you soon."

We cut the lights in the library. Me and Anthony and Will wait by the door. Ms. Curtis, Mom, and the other parents snake a line of blindfolded kids slowly up the hall. They're all silent as we lead them to their seats. Then Anthony hits the switch on the disk player, starting the final phase.

"Remove your blindfolds and prepare for Teleporta takeoff," I instruct in my official voice. "Hang on tight," Will adds, while rocket-blastoff sounds overpower the room and a red strobe light begins to flash. Anthony hits another switch and kills the strobe, and a large flat screen instantly lights up in front of the kids.

"Welcome to the Columbia Space-Science Center in Georgia . . ." a voice says. And suddenly Dad's on the screen. "Am I coming in okay, Stuey?"

"Loud and clear, Dad. How about us?"

"Have Anthony switch the light on,

CONTROL PANEL

that's better . . ." He waves and says, "Hi, kids!"

"Is that man your real father, Stuey Lewis? He can't actually see us, can he? Did you and Will plan all this? Is *he* the space surprise?"

Dad laughs. "I bet you're Lilly, and yes, I am Stuey's *real* dad *and* the space surprise. Thanks to the Internet, computers, Skype, and the webcams Anthony set up, I can see and hear each one of you perfectly."

"No way," says Sam.

"Awesome," Nathan says.

"So, how about we get this field trip started . . . Ready to explore the space center?" Dad asks.

"Yes!" everyone yells. And me and Anthony and Will look at each other and smile.

First stop is the *Challenger* exhibit, where Dad takes us all inside a rocket and simulates a launch. Then we're off to the observatory, where there's a giant telescope and we get to see close-up shots of the Milky Way and Andromeda galaxies. Finally, we take a movie trip through the solar system in the Omni Theater.

"Thanks for coming to visit with me," Dad says after we've been glued to the screen for almost two hours.

"That was the best field trip ever," says Sashi.

"It sure was," Ms. Curtis agrees. "How about a big thank-you cheer for Stuey, Will, and Stuey's family for making this all happen."

"Hurray!" everyone yells, and I give Dad a double thumbs-up.

"Before I sign off, I have one more

surprise for you," Dad says. Anthony and Will look at me, but I'm as clueless as everybody else. "It won't happen just yet, it will be around midnight," he promises.

"Are you referring to the second moon pie treats I'm planning to serve later, Mr. Lewis?" Lilly asks.

"No, but I wish you could teleport one," he says with a grin.

"Well, I can't imagine anything more exciting than *this* happening tonight," says Ms. Curtis.

"Just you wait," Dad says, "and keep your eye on the sky tonight, guys. Anthony, Stu, I'll call you on Sunday." He waves. "Bye, Ms. Curtis. Bye, kids, and don't forget to look up!"

"Bye!" we all say, waving back. Then Anthony hits a switch and the screen turns off.

"I can't believe it's midnight and we're all still awake," says Rosa from her sleeping bag.

"Well, almost all of us," says Will, poking his dad, who's starting to snore.

"I never stay up this late." Ms. Curtis yawns.

"I don't, either," says Mom.

"What do you think the bonus space surprise is?" Anthony asks.

"No idea," I answer.

"Maybe we'll see a UFO after all," says Sam, staring up at the inky-black night.

"You can't possibly think you're going to see an alien ship in the sky, Sam Baker," Lilly says. "Whoa! Did anyone see that? Look, over there!" She points. "There's another one! What *is* that?"

I look up and catch the tail of a

falling light before it fades out. And then I see two more, and I can't believe this night could be any better.

"It's an IFO," I say, "as in . . . Identified Falling Object."

"What are you talking about, Stuey Lewis?" Lilly asks, as more bright lights fire across the sky.

"The bonus surprise is a meteor shower!" I tell everyone.

"Maybe you should call your dad to make sure," Lilly suggests.

"Why don't you just lie back and enjoy the light show," I say.

Then I hunker down in my sleeping bag, gaze up at all the shooting stars, and think, For the rest of tonight, *please* give . . . me . . . space.

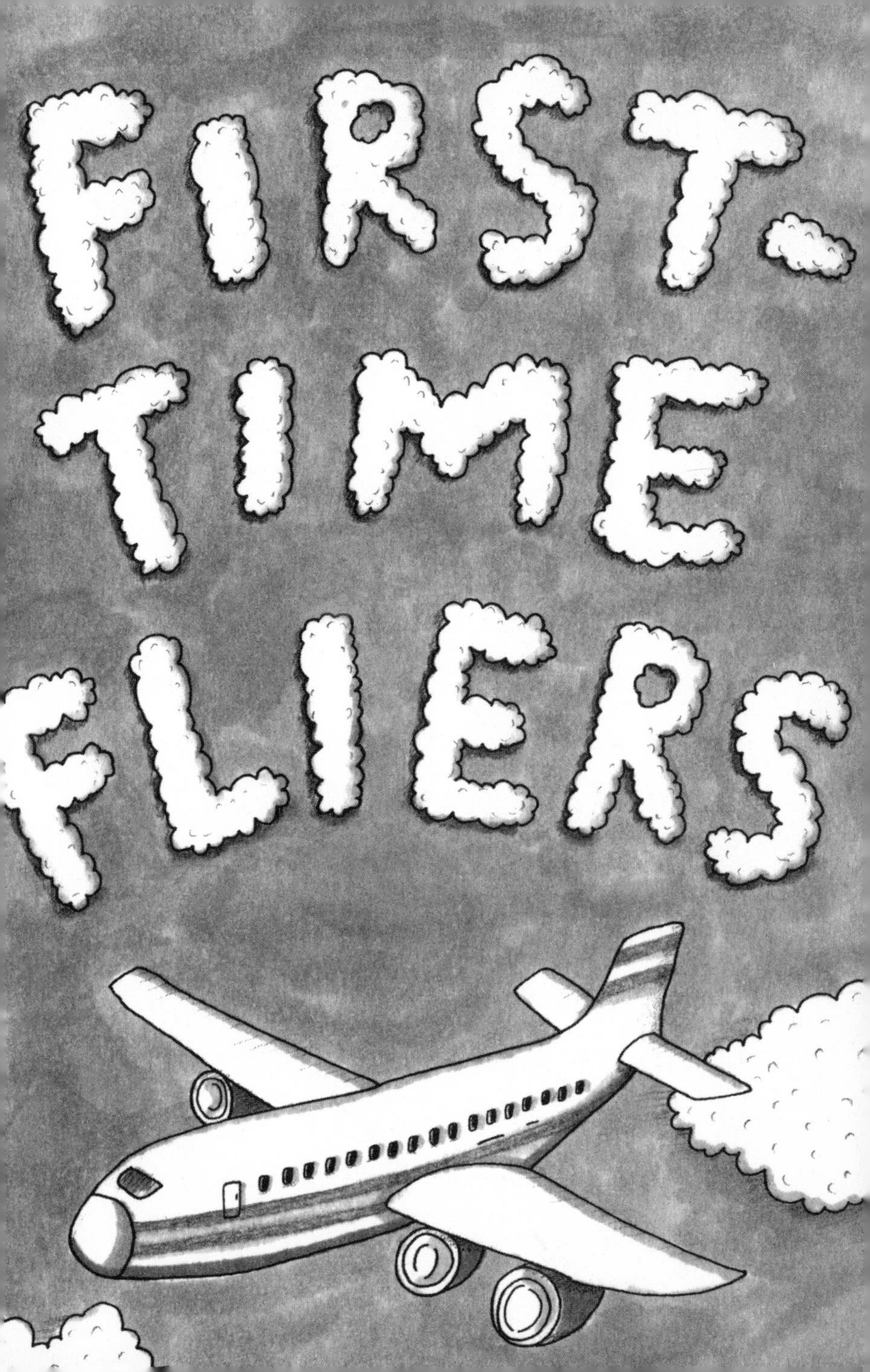
FIRST-TIME FLIERS

Ten minutes until winter vacation!" Ms. Curtis is definitely in holiday mode. Fuzzy antlers stick out of her head, and she's wearing a shiny red nose that blinks on and off. She gives me a paper bag with my name on it. Inside are my presents for Mom and Dad. Pinecones stuffed with peanut butter and sunflower seeds, with red ribbons attached. They're bird feeders, for outside.

"Let's have a quick share about holiday plans and wishes," she calls.

"My twin cousins are coming to visit for three days with their dog, Buster," says Sashi. "I want a girl dog just like him.

So I'm wishing for a white puppy with black spots."

"Well, then, Sashi," says Lilly, "*you* need to wish for a dalmatian."

"I wish for a pair of hockey skates," says Omar. "My big brother plays hockey, and my dad turns our back lawn into a skating rink every year when the weather gets cold enough."

"We're going to my grandpa's in the country," says Sam. "I wish for snow."

"You wish for *snow* for Christmas?" Lilly rolls her eyes. She looks at Sam like he's a big dweeb. "*I* wish for a slushie maker. And a glitter kit. And an extra wish."

If I had an extra wish, I'd make the president of the know-it-alls disappear . . . Poof! Just like that! *Forever.*

"I wish that everyone had food and there was no more war," says Will.

Trust me, this is not because Hanukkah's halfway over and Will's already got four presents. He really means it. No lie.

"And you, Stuey?" Ms. Curtis asks.

"I wish I was cloned."

Lilly snickers. She's not the only one.

"That's a very interesting wish, Stuey," says Ms. Curtis. "Would you like to tell us why?"

Luckily the bell rings, so I don't have to.

"Have a great holiday, everybody. See you all next year!" Ms. Curtis says. She hands each of us a candy cane on our way out the door.

"So, Stu, what's up with your wish?" Will asks me as we're leaving school. "Do you really want to be cloned?"

I nod.

"For real?"

I close my eyes and try to imagine two of me having to put up with Lilly Stanley. It's a very scary thought.

"Okay, forget cloning," I say to him. "I

have a better idea. I'll give up Christmas. Next year, I'll only celebrate Hanukkah, like you."

"How come?"

"So I can spend four days of it with Mom and the other four with Dad."

Will nods. "Cool idea. If you come over now, I'll give you our extra menorah."

That Will, he's the best friend ever.

When I get home, I ask Anthony if he thinks Santa will be mad if we decide to celebrate Hanukkah instead of Christmas.

"I don't get it," he says. "What's this all about, Stu?"

"Mom's been acting sad all week. We have to leave for Dad's tomorrow. It's gonna be really hard."

"I know it is," Anthony agrees, "but we've got to stick with the new routine. Mom had us for Thanksgiving this year, so Dad gets us for Christmas."

"But we won't get to see Mom for a *wicked* long time."

"We haven't seen Dad for a long time, either," says Anthony. "Not since we went camping this summer, and we've never even been to his new home."

"It just stinks that he has to live so far away," I say.

"Big-time," says Anthony.

"But listen, if we decided to celebrate Hanukkah from now on, we could spend half the holiday with each of them. What do you think?"

"You know, Stu, it's not like it's a really *bad* idea . . ." I can tell he doesn't want to hurt my feelings, which, trust me,

44

doesn't happen too often. "It's just not a really *good* one." He puts his arm around my shoulders. "Don't worry, Mom will be okay," he says. "And so will we."

"Thanks, Anthony," I say.

"Hey, guys!" Mom calls. "It's time for us to celebrate Christmas."

We run down the stairs. The tree's all lit, with a pile of presents under it. I look at the fireplace. Our stockings aren't there.

"We'll pack your stockings," says Mom. "Santa will know where to find you." She gives me a wink. "He'll bring the rest of your presents there, too."

I get a wizard's kit with a wand but no rabbit. I get some books and the Lego set I wanted. Me and Anthony save our biggest packages for last. We each get a small suitcase that has wheels and a handle that pulls up.

"You can roll these right onto the plane, boys." Mom tries to sound excited, but it doesn't work. "Your suitcase won't get lost if it's with you."

I give her my presents. She loves the pinecone but looks a little funny when she sees the menorah.

"What's this for?" she asks.

I explain about switching holidays next year. She gives me a big hug.

"I'll be fine," she says. "Come on, guys, let's have dinner. We've got to get you both packed up and into bed early tonight. We'll need a jump start on tomorrow, it's going to be a long day."

It's kinda quiet at the table, and it's not just because we're chewing steak, which keeps our mouths pretty busy. So I decide to start a conversation and ask a question that's been nagging at me.

"Mom, why don't you come to Georgia with us tomorrow?"

Anthony gives me a kick under the table and a look that tells me I better zip it. *Right now.*

"Oh, I don't think that would be such a good idea, Stuey," she says.

"But—"

Anthony kicks me again. Wicked hard this time, and dead on. If my knee was a football at half field, it would be an instant field goal. *Easy.*

"You know the plans have already been made, Stu," he says quickly, before I have time to scream or tell on him. "So we don't need to talk about it. Mom's going to Aunt Martha's after she drops us off at the airport, we go to Dad's, and you, Mom, and I will all be back together, here, in a week."

Mom grabs her plate and gets busy with cleanup. "I'll only be a phone call away," she tells us. "How about dessert?"

"It's almost time to go, boys," Mom says the next morning. "Come have a waffle."

No way am I eating. When Will flew on a plane, he threw up. So I'm flying on empty first time out.

We get to the airport. It's *humongous*.

We check in at the airline counter, and a smiley lady asks, "First-time fliers? Traveling alone?" We nod. She sticks a name tag on each of us and gives Mom special permission to take us to the gate. Then she promises her we won't get lost. I hope she knows what she's talking about.

"This won't hurt a bit," says a man with a metal detector.

My doctor said that once. *Before* she gave me a shot. She lied. I hold my breath. The man waves a stick around me, but I don't feel a thing. My wand's in my outside suitcase pocket, and I think about waving it back at him to see if he'll disappear. But I'm afraid he'll take it away, so I don't. Then our suitcases get X-rayed.

"I see a Christmas stocking in there." The man gives a little chuckle. "Think Santa will be able to find it?"

"Of course he will," answers Anthony. "You found it, didn't you?"

The man turns red. He opens my suitcase. He unwraps Dad's pinecone and messes up my underwear.

We walk to the gate, and soon it's time to board the plane. Anthony squeezes my hand. Mom squeezes his . . . and I squeeze hers. Mom works hard to look brave. So do we.

She gives us each a pack of bubble-gum. "Chew when you take off and when you land. Be sure to chew hard so your ears don't pop."

Ears pop? What does she mean, *ears pop?* But I don't have time to ask 'cause a lady is taking

us away. She's rolling our suitcases down a ramp.

"Stay with the lady who meets you at the next airport!" Mom yells. "She'll put you on the next plane. Are you listening, boys? Don't forget to stay with the lady!"

Mom sounds kinda freaked out. Want to know a secret? So am I.

The lady hands us over to Kelly, the flight attendant who meets us at the end of the ramp. We say hi to the pilots and check out the cockpit. Kelly shows us to our seats, and I take my wand out of my suitcase and stash it in the seat pocket in front of me. Then she brings us soda and pretzels, all before anyone else gets on the plane! I almost forget about being scared. But then I remember.

"Can popped ears get fixed?" I ask Anthony.

Anthony opens up his bubblegum and puts a piece in his mouth. "Start chewing and you won't have to find out," he tells me.

I chew. The plane fills up with people. I keep chewing, and then we take off. I chew like crazy. My ears don't pop! But my jaw sure feels like it's gonna. I look out the window. I'm flying! Straight up into the sky, right through the clouds! It's not even scary. I'm having such a good time I don't notice how quiet Anthony is. Or how green his face is getting.

"I think I'm going to be sick," he groans.

I think about the two waffles he ate for breakfast. Then I think about Will.

"Will says there's a barf bag in every seat pocket." My hand fumbles around. I pull out the bag just in time.

Anthony heaves, but he's right on target. It all goes in the bag. But now *my* stomach is starting to feel a little funny. When Kelly hurries over to help Anthony, I grab my wand and make a break for the bathroom.

I splash cold water on my face and take a couple of deep breaths. I wave my wand around and say, "I'm not gonna throw up. I'm not gonna throw up." And guess what? I don't. I even start to feel pretty good. Good enough to check out the bathroom, which is as cool as Will said it was. I can't figure out how they fit so much stuff in such a small space. But I do figure out how to flush the toilet, just in case I have to use it later.

When I go to leave the bathroom, the door is stuck and I can't get it open. I wave my wand around again and say, "Open says me! Open says me!" But the door won't budge. The bathroom feels like it's getting smaller, and I just want to get out *now*. I set my wand down and start banging on the door with both my hands. Ever been on an airplane? Then you know it's noisy . . . *real* noisy. I bang as loud as I can. Finally, there's a voice on the other side of the door.

"Do you need help in there?"

"I can't get out!" I scream.

"It's going to be okay. I want you to take a deep breath and calm down. Can you do that for me?" I nod. "Okay then," the voice goes on. "Now, do you see where the door lock is?" I nod again. "Move the door lock to the right!"

And just like that . . . I escape. Kelly hands me a cup of water.

"Are you all right?" she asks.

"Sure," I lie, taking a sip. "Can I go back to Anthony now?"

Then she walks me down the aisle to my seat, while everyone on both sides stares at me and smiles. But I'm too busy being invisible to smile back.

It must be a lot of work flying, 'cause both me and Anthony are totally wiped out by the time our plane lands. And we have to do it all over again in two hours. We roll our suitcases off the plane. A lady is standing right there to meet us.

"Anthony and Stuart Lewis?" She checks our name tags. "I'm Carmen.

Until your next plane takes off, you boys need to stay with me at all times. Understand?"

We nod. We know the drill. Mom told us, *ten* times . . . at least.

"How about some pizza?" Carmen asks.

Sounds good to me. Anthony looks like he can handle it, too.

"Can I go to the bathroom first?" I ask. I point. "It's right over there."

"Okay," she says. "We'll wait for you *right here*. Come back as soon as you're done."

I scoot into the bathroom. I check out the door locks. I breathe easy. This is a place I can deal with. When I'm done, I wash my hands. And then I remember my wand. I left it on the plane! I run out of the bathroom. Anthony and Carmen are looking in the other direction, and they don't see me. But the gate is just in front of me. If I hurry, I'll be back in a flash.

I bolt down the ramp, but I get stuck behind a family. They crawl along like snails. Each of them has a suitcase with wheels. I guess they don't want their stuff to get lost, either. It takes forever to get back on the plane.

"Welcome aboard," Kelly greets the family. When she sees me, she frowns. "Stuey? What are you doing here? Aren't you flying to Atlanta, Georgia?"

I nod.

"Well, this is a through-flight, we're continuing on to Denver, Colorado."

"I forgot my magic wand," I tell her. "I left it in the bathroom."

"Don't move," she says. More people

get on the plane. It's a while before she's back.

"Is this it?" She hands me my wand.

"Thanks," I say, and turn to go.

"Does anyone know you're here, Stuey?"

"My pizza's getting cold. Gotta run," I tell her. And I'm off.

I get to the end of the ramp. I'm out of the gate. I see the bathroom. I look all around.

"Stay with the lady." I hear Mom's voice in my head. But there is no lady. No Anthony. No suitcases. No nothing.

It's okay. Everything is okay. Pizza. I bet they're eating pizza and Anthony got me pepperoni. And they're waiting for me to come and get it. I just have to find them. But I can't ask anyone, 'cause Mom says *never, ever* talk to strangers.

Beep-beep! The driver of a cart calls, "Out of the way, please." He's wearing a uniform and he's got a name tag, just like me.

I take a chance. "Do you work here?"

"Yes, I do, young man. I drive people and suitcases to different areas of the airport."

"Do you know where the pizza place is?" I ask.

"Which one?"

"There's more than one?"

"There are four, including the kiosks."

"Four?" My stomach does a backflip.

"Where's your mom or dad?" he asks.

"Mom's back home, and Dad's waiting for us in Georgia," I answer.

"Well, then, who are you traveling with?"

"Anthony, my big brother."

The man looks around. "I don't see him. Where is he?"

"Eating pizza with the lady who's gonna put us on the next plane."

He checks me out. "Young man, are you lost?" he asks.

Lost? How can *I* be *lost?* I look to the left. I look to the right. And then it hits me. There are a million people walking around and *four* places to get pizza in this airport. How am I ever gonna find Anthony? How is he ever gonna find me? *I'm lost!*

I open up my mouth. *"Anthony!"* I scream as loud as I can. *"Anthony!"*

I close my eyes. I wave my wand. But he doesn't appear.

"Don't worry," says the man. "Get in and we'll go find him."

"I can't," I say.

"Why not?" he asks.

"Mom says never get in a car with a stranger."

The man nods. "Your mom sounds like a smart lady. Okay then, I'm going to call Security on my cell phone. Do you think you can tell me your name?"

"Stuey Lewis," I say. I'm trying hard not to cry.

He makes the call. He looks at me the

whole time he's talking. He signs off and smiles at me.

"Well, Stuey Lewis, you are a pretty famous fellow. A lot of people have been looking for you. And they are very happy to hear that you are safe."

"What about my brother?" I ask. "Is he safe, too?"

"Why don't you ask him yourself?" The man points to a cart that's driving toward us.

"Anthony!" I holler. I wave and jump up and down so he can see me.

"Stuey!" he hollers back.

And then we're hugging each other. And even though I'm trying real hard not to, I cry.

We stay with the lady. She puts us on the next plane. Our ears don't pop.

We drink more soda and we eat more pretzels. Only this time Anthony doesn't throw up and I don't get locked in the bathroom. Before we know it, the pilot is talking.

"Fasten your seat belts. We'll be landing in Atlanta, Georgia, in about fifteen minutes."

Finally, we're on the ground. We roll our suitcases off the plane. Anthony's squeezing my hand so tight it hurts. And then we see him.

Dad! we both shout. He picks us up at the same time and twirls us around. He feels like home.

"Let me look at you." He puts us down, takes a step back, and checks us out. "You guys look great! You've grown at least a foot since July. I've missed the two

of you so much." He gives us each a kiss. "So, tell me, how was your first flight?"

Me and Anthony sneak a peek at each other.

"Pretty smooth," says Anthony.

"Yeah," I say. *"Pretty* smooth."

"Well, we'd better call your mom right away," Dad says. "She'll want to know that you got here safely. Then we'll go home and bake Christmas cookies for Santa." He gives me a wink. "Chocolate chip or peanut butter?" he asks.

"How about both?" I answer.

"Sounds good to me," says Dad.

"Me, too," says Anthony. And then we're off to find Dad's car and see our new home in Georgia, which turns out to be closer than I thought.

Just a couple of flights away.

Hey, Stu." Anthony grabs me on my way down to Sunday pancakes. "How much money have you got saved up?" he whispers.

"Not much. I just spent most of it on Easter candy for Will."

"But Will doesn't celebrate Easter," Anthony says. "And Easter was a while ago."

"Duh, the leftover stuff was less than half price. Will has a thing for Marshmallow Peeps, so I got him a ton, and I got some for me, too. They're a little hard, but they still taste pretty good. Do you want one? Yellow or pink?" I pull a couple out of my pocket and give him my most generous smile.

"You spent your money on stale Peeps? That's just great, Stu-pid. How much do you have left?"

"Seventy-three cents, and quit calling me Stu-pid, lamebrain. So, what's up with all the money questions?"

"I thought we could pool our cash together and get something nice for Mom for Mother's Day. But I guess I thought wrong."

"Come on, Anthony, I forgot all about Mother's Day. Why do you want to go in with me in the first place?"

Anthony's face goes red. "Steven asked me for the five dollars I owe him. He needs it to buy a gift for his mom. So, I have to give it to him. I only have two dollars and sixty cents left," he says quietly.

Steven Roy is Anthony's best friend. They borrow everything from each other . . . even socks, but not underwear. He's as close to Anthony as Will is to me. Steven wouldn't have asked for the money unless he had to.

"We could still put our money together and get her one of those big chocolate bunnies," I suggest. "I saw a couple left at the drugstore the other day."

"Oh, that's just brilliant, Stuey," he says, rolling his eyes.

"It's not such a bad idea, Anthony, you know how much Mom loves chocolate."

"Look, leftover Easter candy doesn't cut it for me, but, hopefully, one of us will come up with a better plan by Friday. Otherwise, I think we should each go solo. It will look way too pathetic if we both go in on a cheesy gift."

"I'll do my best," I tell him.

"Boys!" Mom calls to us from downstairs. "Your pancakes are getting cold. Get a move on."

Dad phones me later. "Don't forget Mother's Day next Sunday."

"Yeah, Anthony already reminded me this morning."

"Good, I'm glad to see you boys are so on top of things."

"How come there's a Mother's Day *and* a Father's Day?" I ask him. "There's a Grandparents Day, too. There's even a Teachers' Day and a Secretary's Day. So how come there's no Kid's Day?"

"Stuey, *every* day is Kid's Day," Dad says. "Think about it. Your mom brings you to soccer practice, watches your games, buys you what you need, and takes good care of you. I bet she even made you and Anthony Sunday pancakes this morning, didn't she?"

"Yeah."

"Then you know what I mean. I'll call you next week, okay?"

"Okay," I say. But I still think not having an official Kid's Day kinda stinks.

* * *

"So, Will," I say on my way into our classroom the next morning, "what are you giving your mom for Mother's Day?"

"I don't know," he says. "My dad usually gets her something from all of us. Last year we gave her flowers and took her out for dinner. Moms love that kind of stuff."

"Flowers *and* out to dinner, huh?" I do the math. "What else do moms love that doesn't cost so much?"

"Got a money problem, Stu?" he asks.

"Big-time," I answer.

"Sorry I can't help," he says. "I spent my last three dollars at Paperback Heaven. But Ginger might have an idea."

Of course! Ginger will have a zillion

ideas. She's all about holidays. We'll probably spend the whole week making presents for our moms. Who needs money when I've got my teacher to save me? Monday is suddenly looking up.

I take a deep breath and relax for the first time all morning.

"Guess what I got my mom for Mother's Day," Lilly yells, running up to Sashi from across the room.

Believe me, it's tough staying relaxed when the most irritating girl on earth happens to be in your class.

"It's the best present ever, Sashi!" Lilly is jumping up and down. "It's a heart necklace that opens. I saved and saved to buy it. But it was definitely worth it. Mother's Day *is* only once a year. And guess what I put inside? The cutest picture of her and me! My mom is just going to flip when she sees it."

Lilly is so happy she looks like she might burst. It makes me want to stick a pin in her . . . Sashi looks like she might like to stick a pin in her, too.

"Well, friends," says Ms. Curtis. "Mother's Day is just what I wanted to discuss with you. Can you all join me in the meeting area?"

I look at Ms. Curtis and wait to be rescued.

"We're going to do something *very* special for your moms this year. Here's the plan. We'll have a Mother's Day Tea next Monday, with flowers on the tables. We'll make fancy place mats, and we'll serve tea and treats that we'll be baking here, at school, all this week. And we'll sing songs for them, too."

"Oh, Ginger, you've done it again!" says Lilly. "My mom would just love to come to a tea party!"

"I think my mom would like it, too," Omar says. "But she'll have to leave work early."

"My mom's favorite thing to drink is tea," says Sam.

"My mom loves brownies," says Nathan. "Can we make those?"

"Can my grandma come instead?" asks Rosa. "She's also a mom, and I don't think my mom can miss work."

"That's a good point," says Ms. Curtis. "Of course you can invite a grandmother. You can invite any special someone that takes care of you. Are there any more comments?" She looks right at me.

"It sounds okay," I say. "But what are

we *really* gonna give them? What's the *real* present we're gonna make for our moms?"

"Duh," says Lilly. "The tea party *is* the present, Stuey Lewis. Don't you get it?"

Will jumps right in. "The tea party is a great idea, Ginger. But are we also going to make gifts for our moms?"

"I don't think there will be time for that, Will," she says. "We'll have way too much to do to get ready for the party, besides our schoolwork." Then she looks right at me again. "I thought that might be enough."

Well, guess what? It's not. Not enough to rescue me from my problem. Not even close. But then my brain kicks into overdrive.

"What if we have the tea party on

Sunday?" I ask, with my best smile. "That way it will be a *real* Mother's Day Tea."

"But I can't come on Sunday," says Lilly. "We're going to my grandma's house. She lives far away."

"We'll miss you," I say. I'm so desperate I almost mean it.

"I can't do it, either," says Rosa. "My cousins are coming over."

"The school's closed Sunday, and I've got family plans, too, so it won't work, but it was a good thought, Stuey," Ms. Curtis says.

But not good enough. So now what am I gonna do?

The minute I get home from school, Anthony asks, "Have you figured out what to get Mom yet?"

"Ginger had this idea," I tell him. "We're having a Mother's Day Tea next

Monday. It's a pretty big deal. We've already started working on it. Have a look at the invitation."

I take out the yellow envelope with teacup stickers. *Mom* is spelled out in my very best cursive, in silver-glitter ink. Even though it's pretty girly, it looks kinda cool.

Anthony's face is a little funny. But I'm not sure what kind of funny. Finally, his lips unzip.

"Well, I guess you don't need me after

all," he mumbles. "Looks like you've got Mom all covered now."

"But the tea thing doesn't really count," I say. "It's the day after Mother's Day and it's from all the kids in the whole class, not just from me. And it's for everybody else's mother, too."

"At least it's something," Anthony says. "Mom will totally be into it. I wish our class could have a special party like that, but you don't get to do holidays in seventh grade."

I check him out to see if he's kidding. But he's not.

"Look, Anthony, we still have five whole days to come up with an idea. Let's make a pinkie swear to do something together for Mother's Day, no matter what." I put my arm around him and say, "Don't worry, I know we can pull something off."

Anthony smiles and holds out his little finger. "Got any more Peeps in your pocket?"

I hand him a yellow one. Then we lock pinkies.

On Friday afternoon we split into groups to finish up details for the party. Will's group gets to complete the giant **MOM** banner. But I have to work with Lilly, decorating

empty soup cans that Ms. Curtis says will look just perfect filled with flowers. Covering soup cans with colored paper is not as easy as it sounds. Trust me. You have to line up the paper and cut it just right so it doesn't stick out on top of the can. Then it has to be glued *very* neatly, which takes *a lot* of patience and *not* a lot of glue.

Did I mention that it has nothing to do with fun and that you need a wicked long time to do just one? Lilly finishes four by the time I finish mine. But who's counting?

"Maybe you could make an extra one to give to your mom as a present," whispers Will.

"Maybe I'd rather get chicken pox or head lice," I whisper back.

Ms. Curtis looks around the room as the bell rings. "It's a wrap, friends. Our sweets are in the freezer, we know our songs, our place mats are made, and now our decorations are complete. We're all set to celebrate on Monday. I'm proud of you all. Your moms work hard every day taking care of you, and you've worked hard all week to make your moms feel like queens for a day."

Queens for a day . . .

Queens for a day . . .

Bingo! Ginger saved me after all. If you take the *s* off *queens*, you end up with *queen*. One mom can be a queen for a day. And me and Anthony are just the right guys to crown Mom.

"Have a great weekend," Ms. Curtis says. I give her a giant grin.

Then I high-five Will. "You figured something out, huh?" he says. "I knew you would."

When I get home, I pull Anthony up to my room. "Sunday's gonna be the best day of Mom's whole life," I tell him.

"You've got a plan?"

I lay out the details.

"It's killer," he says. "Maybe your best one yet." And then he high-fives me. "Stuey Lewis to the rescue!"

Before lunch on Saturday, Anthony slips into my room, closing the door behind him. "After Steven's track meet this morning, we went with his mom to the

85

party store to get balloons for his sister's birthday," he tells me. "Guess what I found?" He dangles a crown in front of my face. It's gold and has sparkly stuff glued all over it.

"Wow! It's a beaut," I whisper.

"It cost two dollars." He looks kinda worried.

"It doesn't matter. We don't need any more money," I tell him. " 'Cause everything else we give Mom is stuff we're gonna *do* for her." I hand him the list I've been working on. "Here are a few ideas I thought we could start with."

QUEEN-FOR-A-DAY LIST
1. Bring Mom breakfast in bed.
2. Get her a Scoops ice cream treat.
3. Share Easter candy.
4. Dinner?

Anthony reads the list out loud. Then he takes a pencil and makes some changes.

QUEEN-FOR-A-DAY LIST
1. Crown Mom queen for a day.
2. ~~1.~~ Bring Mom breakfast in bed.
3. ~~2. Get her a Scoops ice cream treat.~~ Wash Mom's car, then go to Suds and vacuum it.
4. ~~3. Share Easter candy.~~ Go grocery shopping with Mom.
5. ~~4. Dinner?~~ Have a picnic.

"Breakfast in bed is perfect," he says. "But now that we bought her a crown, we don't have enough money to go to Scoops." I nod. "So, listen, Stu. The Peeps work for you. And maybe they even work for me . . . But they won't really work for Mom. Agree?" I nod again.

"Mom always buys groceries on Sundays, so we can go with her to help. And if you and I wash the car at home first, we'll have just enough quarters to pay for the power vacuum at Suds to clean the inside of it." I give him a thumbs-up. "And I bet if we throw hot dogs and buns in the cart while we're at the market, Mom will buy them. Then we can put them on the grill and make a picnic for her. What do you think?"

"I think two heads are better than one," I say. Then I give him and me a noogie to demonstrate my point.

"We can pull this off, Stu," he says. "But we can't let Mom know anything. Not until we give her the crown first thing in the morning."

"Mum's the word," I say. "Get it?"

Anthony laughs. "Tomorrow's going to be so cool."

"It's gonna be the best day of her whole life," I say.

I get up wicked early Sunday morning. Even before Anthony. I sneak into the kitchen and get started on my specialty breakfast. I put the flower I picked from Mom's garden on her tray. I use the fancy dishes from the dining room. I work carefully and quietly. I'm just about finished when Anthony shows up.

"I can't believe it! You made Mom a fluffernutter for breakfast?"

"Of course," I say. "It *is* Mother's Day. Shouldn't she get the best breakfast to start the best day of her whole life?"

Anthony looks like he wants to say something, but he doesn't.

"Why don't you pour Mom a glass of milk," I say. "We're just about ready. What time is it, anyway?"

"Only six o'clock," he says. "We've got plenty of time before Mom gets up. How about we make her a fruit salad with yogurt to go with the sandwich?"

"Nice touch," I say.

We put the crown and everything else on the tray. I let Anthony carry it upstairs. We wait by her door till we hear her get up.

"Stay where you are! Don't move! Don't get out of bed!" we scream, walking in.

"Is everything okay? What's going on?" Mom looks totally freaked.

I put the crown on her head. "We

crown you queen for a day! Happy Mother's Day!" Then we give her the tray.

"Wow! Breakfast in bed, and you made all my favorites." She takes a bite of the sandwich. "Thanks, boys, I feel like a real queen."

"Just you wait," I say.

After we clean the dishes, me and Anthony start soaping up the car. I point the hose at it and wait for Anthony to turn the water on.

"Hold on, Stuey!" Mom yells from the house.

I turn around just as the water goes up the hose. Mom gets soaked.

"Ahh!" she screams. Then she starts laughing. "I only wanted to tell you that the rear window is open," she says. "Didn't want the inside of the car to get drenched." Her hair is dripping wet, but her crown

is still on her head. "Guess I'd better change before we go to the store."

"Sorry, Mom," I say.

"I've heard that queens often have two showers a day," she says. "Sometimes even three." She smiles and goes into the house.

"Nice going, Stu," Anthony says as he rolls up the window.

Five minutes later, the car sits gleaming in the driveway.

"You guys are really spoiling me," Mom says. "The car looks fantastic."

"After we get the groceries, can we go to Suds Car Wash?" Anthony asks her. "Stuey and I are going to power vac the inside of the car so everything will be super clean."

Mom's all smiles. "You two have thought of everything."

Anthony turns around and gives me a wink.

Everyone stares at Mom's head in the grocery store. It's as if no one ever saw a queen before. You can tell this is definitely the best day of her whole life. Then she gives Anthony and me a list of stuff to get. Hot dogs and buns aren't on it.

We get everything and bring it back to Mom. Then Anthony and I go off to find the hot dogs. The buns are close by. At the end of the aisle is a giant pyramid of cans.

"Baked beans?" I ask.

"Sure," he says. "I'll get some marshmallows and meet you."

I reach out and grab a can. "Great idea!" I call after him.

Within seconds, a zillion cans of beans

are tumbling down and rolling all over the place.

"Are you okay?" the grocery guy asks me. I nod. "Whose kid is this?" he yells, just as Mom shows up.

I put the beans in her cart. But what I'd really like to put in there is *me*. And then be immediately rolled out the back door.

"Can we check out now?" I ask.

Anthony is already by the door, pretending he doesn't know me.

When we get in the car, Mom says, "Going to the store's not usually so exciting. This has really been a full day. Are you *sure* you still want to go to Suds?"

"It'll be a quick stop. Then we'll head home. We have a surprise planned for later," Anthony says. He gives Mom a look that says, Nothing else can possibly go wrong.

I notice Mom's crown is a bit crooked. Kinda like her smile.

We pull up to the vacuum machine at Suds. It looks like a robot with a giant arm. Anthony hops out and dumps quarters into its mouth. He opens up the car door, hands me the power vac, and flips the switch.

Whirr! The vacuum sucks everything off the back floor in no time flat. Somehow it gets away from me and goes for the groceries.

"It ate the buns! It's heading for the marshmallows!" I yell.

Anthony tries to grab the vac, but Mom gets in his way. Her crown is sucked off her head and instantly swallowed. Then her hair starts to go.

"Turn it off!" she screams.

And just like that, the whirring stops.

Our quarters have run out. The vac is powerless. We look at each other. Mom's hair is pretty messy. Suddenly, she seems really tired.

"Sorry about your crown, Mom." Anthony fixes her hair.

"Are there any hot dog buns in the freezer?" I ask.

"Hot dog buns in the freezer?" Mom repeats.

"That's your last surprise," Anthony explains. "Stuey and I are making you a picnic. So you won't have to cook dinner tonight."

"What if we go out for pizza instead?" Mom asks quickly. Then she sweetens the deal. "And, after, we can go to Scoops for sundaes."

"But it's Mother's Day," I say. "We

wanted to make this *whole* day extra-special, just for you."

Mom gives both of us a kiss. "I don't think I could possibly feel any more special. Believe me, this is a day I will never forget. So, please let me make the two of you feel a little special, okay?"

Anthony and I look at each other. "Okay," we say.

Suddenly, Mom seems less tired. "Let's go!" she says, smiling.

I guess Dad was right. Every day is Kid's Day after all.

Will has a thing for fish. You could say his whole family does. They've got three fish tanks in their house, like the giant ones you see in the dentist's office. They've also got a humongous Saint Bernard named Lucy and a parrot they call Sandro, who counts to five in Spanish and answers *hola* when you say hello.

Some kids have all the luck. Me? I've always wanted a pet, but Mom's allergic to *everything* in the *entire* animal kingdom. If she even thinks of fur, feathers, claws, or slimy skin, her eyes get all itchy and she starts sneezing. *Big-time*.

So, when I feel the need to feed or pet something, I go straight to Will's. He lets me adopt Lucy or Sandro for the whole day. I bet he'd like it more if I adopted Arnie, his little brother, for a whole year. But we both know *that's* never gonna happen.

Turns out I'm there, at Will's house, on the big day . . . when the mail comes and Will's entire family flips out.

"It's here!" his dad yells, waving a card in the air. "Our membership has finally arrived! Let's go."

"Can Stuey come?" Will asks.

"Of course," says Will's mom. "Let me just call his mom to make sure it's okay."

"Where are we going?" I ask.

Will gives me a look. The kind that says, Get with the program.

"To the aquarium." He rolls his eyes. "You know, the *brand-new* state-of-the-art aquarium that's *just* opened. Now that we're official members, we get to go whenever we want, for free."

"Cool," I say, even though I'm not half as crazy about fish as he is. When we get to the aquarium, Will's dad gives the lady the card.

"Ah, the Fishman family, how perfect. *Fish*-man, *Fish* . . . Get it?" She stamps everybody's hand. "Drop an anchor and stay awhile!"

"Can we go see the sharks first?" asks Arnie.

"Sharks?" I don't say it, but sharks are not on my top-ten list.

"Please, please, can we?" begs Arnie.

"That's my boy," says Mr. Fishman. He steers us past the tropical fish and makes a beeline for the shark tank.

"There's the great blue!" screams Arnie. He runs up and plasters his face to the glass. "Awesome! Just look at the size of those teeth!"

"No other creature on the whole planet has more powerful jaws than the shark," says Mr. Fishman. "Each jaw has five to fifteen rows of teeth and some are as long as this." He holds up his pinkie. Waving it in my face, he says, "With just one snap, it could bite off a . . ."

My stomach takes a sharp dive. Way, way down to the bottom of my toes. It feels like it doesn't wanna hear anything more about sharks, and, to tell the truth, the rest of me doesn't, either.

"Uh, Mrs. Fishman, can I check out the tropical fish?"

"That's fine," she says. "But stay right there, Stuey. Don't wander off. Will and the rest of us will meet you over there in a few minutes."

Wander off? Me? No way. I'll be happy
as a clam, watching one fish, two fish,
red fish, blue fish.

"Happy Monday! Time for meeting!"
Ms. Curtis waves us over. "Let's start with

a weekend update. Who has something to share?"

"I do! I do!" Lilly's arm goes flying up into the air. The rest of her looks ready for takeoff. "Call on *me*, Ginger! Call on *me, please!*"

"You seem pretty excited this morning, Lilly," Ms. Curtis says calmly. "How come?"

"Bet you can't guess what I got this weekend," she says.

A new personality would be nice, I think to myself. Or maybe a one-way rocket ride to the moon.

"I knew you couldn't guess," she says in her know-it-all voice. "Well, I got a ferret!"

No one says anything.

"Maybe you can tell us what a ferret is," Ms. Curtis says.

"I'm sure you already know the answer to that, Ginger," Lilly says. "But since you asked . . . It's an exotic pet."

"What does *exotic* mean?" asks Sam.

"Unusual," Ms. Curtis says.

Lilly smiles. "That's correct, Ginger. Hardly anybody has a ferret for a pet," she tells us all.

"That's because they smell funny," I say.

"They do not, Stuey Lewis!" Lilly protests.

"Well, they *are* related to the skunk family," I say.

"P-U!" Sashi holds her nose. We all laugh. Lilly's face turns red.

"Any other weekend updates?" Ms. Curtis asks.

"Stuey came with my family to the new aquarium," says Will. "I bought two exotic fish, *plus*, we saw a great blue shark that's only there for a week before they release it back into the ocean." Will looks at Lilly. "Hardly anybody sees a great blue in captivity."

"That must have been awfully exciting," says Ms. Curtis.

Awful is just about right, I think.

"My gerbil, Mitsy, escaped from her cage for two whole days," says Rosa. "But we found her in our bathroom wastebasket."

"Our dog threw up in our bathroom," says Sam. "We think my little sister gave him her double-chocolate cupcake."

"Ugh, gross!" Sashi holds her stomach.

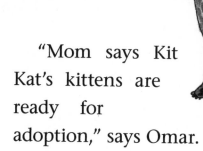

"Mom says Kit Kat's kittens are ready for adoption," says Omar.

"How many of you have pets?" asks Ms. Curtis.

Every single kid raises a hand. Everybody but me and Nathan. I give him my most understanding look. The one that says, I know just how you feel.

"Omar, my dad said we could get a kitten," says Nathan. "Do you think I could adopt one of yours?"

"Sure thing," says Omar.

"I've got an idea," says Ms. Curtis. "I wanted to do something special

BOWWOW BISCUIT

for the end of the school year. I think it would be fun to share our pets, or favorite stuffed animals for those of us that don't have pets or can't bring one in. Who would like to have a pet show?"

Now every single kid, including Nathan, raises a hand. Every kid but me.

"I'll need to ask Ms. Katz," says Ms. Curtis, "but if she says it's okay, we'll have the show next week, the day before school ends. Let's get ready for art."

"So, how come you know so much about ferrets?" Will asks me.

"Dad's friends in Georgia have one. We had fun with her when we were there at Christmas. She could roll over and play fetch. They named her Cha-Cha, 'cause she even learned how to dance."

"No way," Will says. "And do they really smell?"

"Kind of, but only a little. They're actually very cool," I whisper. "And wicked smart. I'd do anything to have one. But don't tell Lilly."

"I checked with Ms. Katz. She says we can have our pet show next Monday," Ms. Curtis announces at the end of the day.

Everyone cheers, except for yours truly.

"But there are some rules we'll need to follow. All big animals must be on a leash. All little animals have to be in something they can't get out of. And a grownup has to come with you and your pet and has to take your pet home after the show." She smiles. "Any questions?"

Yeah, here's one for you: Just how am I supposed to deal with this doggone cat-astrophe?

"Real pet shows give out ribbons or even trophies," Lilly says.

"Do you think we could get prizes?" Sashi asks.

"I'm not sure," says Ms. Curtis. "I thought this would be more about sharing than competing. How do you think you would feel if you didn't win a prize?"

"Maybe we could each win one," Rosa says. "Then nobody would feel left out."

Ding-dong, you're wrong . . . I'm so left out I'm not sure I can find a way in.

Ms. Curtis smiles. "I like your idea, Rosa. I think it's interesting."

Well, guess what? I think it stinks, along with the whole pet-show idea. There's no way I'm bringing in a stupid stuffed animal to school when everyone else is bringing in a live one. I thought third grade was gonna end without a hitch and now, all of a sudden, I have to come up with a pet in *six* days. How am I gonna pull *that* off?

The bell rings. "Have a great afternoon, friends," Ms. Curtis says.

As we pack up to go home, Will says, "Hey, Stuey, I'm going to bring Lucy to the pet show. Want to take some of my fish?"

Ever notice how your best friend can read your mind? Pretty awesome, huh?

"Thanks, Will, but I was hoping for something more exotic."

"More exotic? Reality check, Stu: you have *no* pets."

Ever notice how your best friend can bring you back from la-la land? Just like that. Not so awesome, huh?

"Duh, thanks for the news flash. I know I don't have any pets."

"I was just trying to help." Will sounds kinda upset.

"What's going on with you two?" Ms. Curtis asks.

"Nothing!" we both say at the same time.

"Figure it out yourself, Stu," Will says on his way out the door. "You can bring your teddy bear for all I care."

Ms. Curtis looks at me. "Want to talk?"

"It's the stupid pet show."

"Is that why you're upset with Will?" she asks.

"Will has a ton of pets. Awesome pets, like a Spanish-talking parrot and a giant Saint Bernard. And Lilly's got a ferret.

Even Nathan will have one of Omar's kittens by next week. But I'll have what you get if you multiply 9,876,574 times 0: nothing . . . zilch . . . zip."

"Maybe Will would share one of his pets with you," Ms. Curtis suggests.

"He said I could bring in some of his fish, but I don't think fish are as cool as he does."

"Look, Stuey, I don't have a pet, either. Actually, I was thinking about bringing my stuffed iguana." I roll my eyes at her. "Okay, so that won't work for you, but I know you'll come up with something, you always do. Just use your imagination, you're so good at that, and meanwhile, call Will when you get home to work out this little misunderstanding, okay?"

I get up wicked early on Tuesday to check the homemade trap I set in the backyard last night. It's empty, but I've still got five more days to catch something exotic.

"What are you up to?" Anthony hollers down from his window.

I tell him about the plan Will and I hatched last night on the phone after we made up.

"Stuey, what do you think you're going to catch in a basket? The Easter Bunny? You know, sometimes you cook up some pretty cool schemes. But this isn't one of them."

"So what's *your* brainchild?"

"I don't have one, but maybe Mom can think of something."

"She feels bad enough about her allergies. I don't want Mom to know about this."

"What don't you want Mom to know about?" calls Mom from her window. "And why are you guys up so early?"

Anthony looks down at me. I don't say a word. "We thought we saw an animal back there," Anthony says.

"Yeah," I chime in. "An exotic one."

"An exotic animal? You must be dreaming, but there has been a bunny nibbling on my pansies lately."

Bingo!

Anthony snags me when I come in. "Steven's dad owns a Havahart trap. I'll borrow it, and we'll trap Bugs Bunny tonight, okay?"

It's times like this that make having a big brother worth all the times it isn't. "Anthony Lewis to the rescue," I say.

"Nothing yet," I report to Will as soon as I see him at school. "But there's a rabbit in the garden me and Anthony are gonna trap."

"Well, just in case you don't, I'm working on Plan B," he tells me.

That's why he's still my best friend.

Early Thursday morning, I see it from my window. I run into Anthony's room. "Wake up. We did it! We caught the rabbit! Hurry up, get dressed!" We race downstairs and out the door.

"Sh! Be quiet and move *really* slowly," Anthony whispers. "It's pretty little. We don't want to scare her." We tiptoe over to the trap.

"Uh-oh . . . Is that what I think it is?" I whisper.

"Sure looks like it," says Anthony, taking a step back. Inside is a tiny black-and-white skunk munching away on some lettuce. "We've got to get her out of there, *now.*"

"Not so fast," I say. "It may be a baby, but it's still a skunk."

"I don't think they can spray when they're that small," he says.

I'm not as sure as Anthony, so I take a few steps back when he goes for the cage.

"Be wicked careful, okay?" I whisper, taking more steps back, just in case.

Anthony bends down slowly. He moves so calmly the skunk doesn't seem to know he's even there. He's like invisible. He easily gets the door up in one second and starts to back away. He gives me a grin and a thumbs-up . . . And then we hear Mom.

"Boys! Get out of there, *now*!" She points to a big skunk at the edge of the garden and starts slamming the windows shut.

I just make it to the back door, but Anthony's too late. He's still outside when the skunk lets it rip. It smells like ten stink bombs. And he does, too. I stay home from school to help de-skunk him.

Me and Mom make a mixture of hydrogen peroxide, baking soda, and green dishwashing liquid. Then Mom has Anthony sponge it all over himself and his hair six times in the garage before she lets him in the house.

"I appreciate that you boys were trying to save my pansies from that bunny," she says, "but you never know *what* you're

going to catch when you set those things out. So I think you'd better give Steven's trap back when it doesn't smell anymore, Anthony. I can live with a few less flowers."

* * *

I try not to freak on Friday, waiting for Will to get to school. I grab him the second he walks through the door.

"So Plan A's failed. I can't catch the rabbit, and I'm running out of time." I take a deep breath. "Tell me quick, what's Plan B?"

Will doesn't look happy. "Plan B didn't work, either," he says.

"What do you mean?" I moan.

"I tried to get Mom to let you bring Sandro to school. I even taught him to say *Stuey rules*, but Mom won't budge. She thinks he'll be way too nervous. Sorry, Stu, I did my best."

"It's okay, Will. I know you did."

"You can still take the fish, if you want. You can take the two new ones we got at the aquarium." I don't say anything.

124

"Or any other ones you like. Come over after school and choose a few."

"Thanks, Will."

Ms. Curtis calls out, "Time for meeting, friends! Let's talk a little bit about our plans for Monday." She looks at me when she asks, "Is everybody all set for our pet show?"

"I can hardly wait, Ginger!" says Lilly. "You won't believe the amazing trick I taught my ferret."

"Mitsy's learning how to ring a bell," says Rosa.

"Dad got a brush to make Little Bit look beautiful," says Nathan. "But she's pretty fluffy already."

"Kit Kat will be excited to see her," says Omar.

"We bought pink hair ribbons to put on Tina," says Sashi.

"We're giving Cooper a bath on Sunday," Sam says.

I try to picture myself putting pink hair ribbons on a fish. It doesn't work. Neither does teaching it to ring a bell or play dead. Giving it a bath might, but it probably wouldn't change the way it smelled. Let's face it . . . fish aren't all that exciting.

Just don't tell Will I said that.

When the three o'clock bell rings, I'm wasted. My brain's been working overtime. But my brain has nothing to show for it. I've spent the whole day trying to come up with Plan C. But all I've come up with is Plan F . . . *F* for *fish* . . . *F* for *failed*.

As soon as we get into Will's house, he pulls me over to a tank.

"I just know we'll find you the perfect

fish, Stu. This is my new personal favorite." He points to a shiny blue one. "Isn't she a beauty?"

"How do you know it's a she?" I ask.

"Do you like this one better?" He shows me a silvery-green one with red stripes on its tail. It almost looks electric.

"That one *is* pretty cool-looking," I have to admit.

Will smiles. "Good," he says. "Now we're getting somewhere."

"Does it do anything unusual?" I ask.

"Unusual? Like what?"

"I don't know," I say. *"Anything."*

"It can swim," he says.

"Besides swim."

"Stuey, it's a fish." Will sounds like he's trying to be patient. "What do you want it to do, talk? Play fetch? Sing a song?"

"That would be awesome."

"Well, Stu, I'm sorry to tell you it doesn't do any of those things. It's beautiful and peaceful and if that's not exotic enough for you, then don't take any to the pet show." He turns away from me and the tank and heads down the hall toward his bedroom.

"Will, don't be mad. I'm sorry. I know you're just trying to help, and I'm being stupid." I follow him into his room. "It's just that . . ."

"Arrrrr!" Suddenly, I feel something grab me from behind and it's not letting go. *"Arrrrr!"*

"Cut it out, Arnie!" Will yells. "It's not funny and neither are you. I'm getting really sick of this and if you don't cool it right now, I'm going to tell Mom."

"Arrrrr!"

"That's it! I warned you, Arnie! Mom! He's at it again!"

I whirl around. Arnie's wearing the shark mask he got at the aquarium.

"Arrrrr!" he screams again, and dives under the bed.

Will's mom runs into the room. Will points under the bed, and she kneels down. "Arnold Neal Fishman, if you don't come with me to the kitchen immediately, you're going to end up in the frying pan!"

Arnie shoots out from under the bed. "Arrrrr," he says softly. He follows his mother out of the room.

"What's up with him?" I ask.

"Well, you know how crazy he is about sharks. He's been pretending to be one ever since our trip to the aquarium."

"No way, since last weekend?"

"Yeah, he hasn't taken his mask off yet. Mom says he'll get tired of it soon enough. But for now, he's not Arnie. He's a shark. Pretty crazy, huh?"

I nod. And then I hear Ginger's words in my head: *I know you'll come up with something, you always do. Just use your imagination, you're so good at that.*

I feel a giant grin taking over my face. I've just come up with a plan that's so wacky it might work. I grab Will's hand and pull him toward the kitchen.

I'm still wearing a grin when Mr. Fishman drives me home. I run straight up to Anthony's bedroom and fill him in on my plan.

"I think you just hooked the big one," he says. "Nice catch!"

* * *

I get to school early Monday morning. I'm all set to break pet-show history. I walk into class and give Ms. Curtis the thumbs-up.

She smiles. "You came up with something, huh?"

"It's all about imagination," I say. "It'll be here when Will brings his dog, Lucy, and you're gonna be really surprised when you see it."

"Hm," says Ms. Curtis. "Sounds very mysterious."

"Mysterious *and* exotic," I say.

Lilly walks in with her mom, holding a cage. "Ginger, Stuey, I'd like you to meet Chocolate."

"Nice-looking ferret," I tell her.

"What did you bring?" she asks.

"It's coming soon," I answer.

The room starts filling up with all

kinds of animals and parents. It's getting pretty noisy when I finally see Will signaling to me from the door. I meet him in the hall.

"Hi, Stuey," says Mrs. Fishman. She's got Lucy's leash in one hand and Arnie's hand in the other. "Are you boys ready for your pets? Just remember, you'll have to hold on tightly to keep them under control." She gives the leash to Will. "Here's your dog." Then she puts Arnie's hand in mine. "And, Stuey, here's your shark."

We walk into the classroom. Suddenly, everyone's quiet.

"Whoa, Will has a giant dog!" says Sashi. "Awesome!"

"But what's Stuey have?" asks Lilly.

"Boys," says Ms. Curtis, "would you please introduce your pets?"

"This is Lucy, my Saint Bernard," says Will proudly. "Sit, girl." Lucy sits, and everyone claps.

"And this is Arnie, my shark," I say. "Speak, fish."

"Arrrrr!" roars Arnie, and everyone laughs.

"That is one unique pet," says Ms. Curtis.

"What does *unique* mean?" asks Sam.

"One of a kind," says Ms. Curtis.

"That's for sure," says Lilly.

Then we all parade our pets around the room, and Ms. Curtis takes pictures and gives everyone, including Arnie, a Best-in-Show ribbon.

When I hand over Arnie to Mrs. Fishman, he takes off his mask and gives it to her. Lucy licks him in the face. "I never ever won anything before in my

whole life," Arnie says, waving his ribbon. "Thanks a lot, Stuey."

"Well, what do you think of that?" says Mrs. Fishman, smiling. "I've got my son back."

"Good timing," I say.

"I'll ditto that," says Will.

Arnie waves goodbye and leaves with his mom and the rest of the parents and pets.

"Looks like you've done it again, Stuey," says Ms. Curtis.

"I never had any doubts," says Will.

"Yeah, it turned out after all." I give them both a big grin. "You know, I've had to pull off some crazy schemes this year, but all in all, third grade has felt pretty good."

I look across the room at Lilly, who's flapping her lips nonstop, as usual. After tomorrow, I'll even be able to say I survived *her*.

"But I guess I wouldn't mind having my life be a *little* less complicated for a while," I tell them. "Maybe I'll even try boring."

Now what do you think the odds are of *that* happening anytime soon?

I'd bet a million to one.

8·12

DATE DUE